Danny Doesn't Quit

Written by
Dana Reid

Illustrated by
Mike Motz

Dear Tanner,
Remember to
keep believing
in yourself!
Dana Reid

To my son, Bradley, and to every kid who has ever felt like quitting when things were hard.

Remember to always believe in yourself and to keep trying. You may be surprised by what is possible.

Danny was a curious little boy.
He loved to try new things.
There was just one problem: he never saw anything
through. Every time something got too hard, he quit.

One day, Danny's dad came home
with a baseball mitt and a bat.
"How about it, bud?" he said.
"Want to learn?"

Danny thought about it for a long time.
He did like watching baseball and going to games.
But he was worried. What if he wasn't any good?
Finally, he decided to give it a try.

A few weeks later, Dad brought Danny
to his first baseball practice.

Danny listened closely as the coaches explained
how to swing the bat and hit a baseball.
Finally, it was his turn to try.

Danny set up like the coaches had told him.
He held his bat over his shoulder. He swung . . .
and he missed.

Danny couldn't hit a single ball that was pitched to him.

His frustration grew as he watched the other kids
on the team. They were all better than him.
Every one of them caught and hit the balls with ease.

"I can't do this," Danny told his dad.
"I don't want to play anymore. I want to go home."

"Come on, Danny," Dad replied.
"It's only the first practice. It will get easier.
Why don't you go back out there and keep trying."

So Danny went back out. He caught one or two balls, and
even hit the ball once. But every play was a struggle.

On the way home, Danny said, "I'll never get good at this. Why should I even try?"

Dad shook his head. "Everything takes practice, Danny. The players you watch on TV don't just know how to play. They practice for hours every day. You'll never get good at anything if you don't put in the effort.

It's time you pick something and keep pushing
through even when it feels hard. It is the only way
you will get better."

Danny thought over his dad's words. "I guess I could
keep trying. I just hope I can learn how to play."

That weekend as Danny stepped up to bat at his first game, he felt nervous. His belly flipped and flopped, and he could feel a puddle of sweat forming on his neck. *What if I can't do it?*

Danny focused his energy on the pitcher. When the ball came his way, he swung.

Danny sighed and squared his shoulders.
STRIKE TWO! STRIKE THREE! YOU'RE OUT!
Dropping the bat, Danny trudged to the dugout.
"I'll never be good at this," he sighed.

To his surprise, Danny heard his teammates shouting for him. "It's okay, Danny! That was a good try. You'll get it the next time."

When Danny's next at bat came, he swung hard.

≥ CRACK! ≤

The ball flew toward the outfield.

I did it! Danny thought, an extra boost of confidence charging through him as he raced to first base. *Maybe I* can *get better at baseball.*

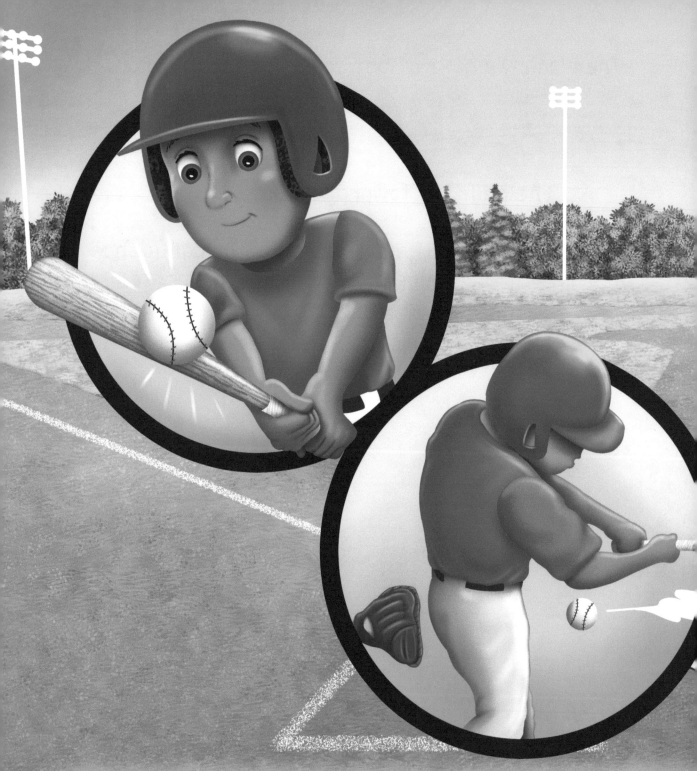

Danny was proud of himself, but he still worried about letting his team down. What if the hit was just a fluke?

"It's not a fluke," his dad said. "You got this, buddy. Believe that you can, and you will!"

Danny wasn't sure he believed that, but he kept trying. Game after game, he tried. Sometimes he hit, and sometimes he struck out. Sometimes he caught the ball and sometimes he dropped it.

After a long season, Danny's team made it
to the championship game.
By the last inning, the teams were tied.
"COME ON, DANNY. IT IS ALL ON YOU, NOW!"
his team screamed as he stepped up to bat.
"BRING IT HOME!"

BALL	STRIKE	OUT
0	0	2

INNING	1	2	3	4	5	6	R
VISITOR	2	0	4	0	0	0	6
HOME	0	5	0	1	0	0	6

Danny took a deep breath and looked around.
They had two outs and bases loaded.
For his team to win, Danny needed to get a hit.

Danny swung at the first two pitches but missed.
He was down to his final strike.

WHAT IF I MISS AGAIN?

Then Danny remembered his dad's words.
Believe that you can, and you will.

Danny took a deep breath
and pictured himself getting a big hit.
As the last pitch was thrown, Danny swung.

CRACK!

He smashed a line drive into the outfield.

Danny grinned as his teammates ran onto the field and carried him away on their shoulders. All around him, the crowd cheered loudly, chanting his name.

Later, as they left the baseball field,
Danny stopped his dad.
"Thank you for pushing me to keep trying.
You were right. I just need to practice
and believe in myself."

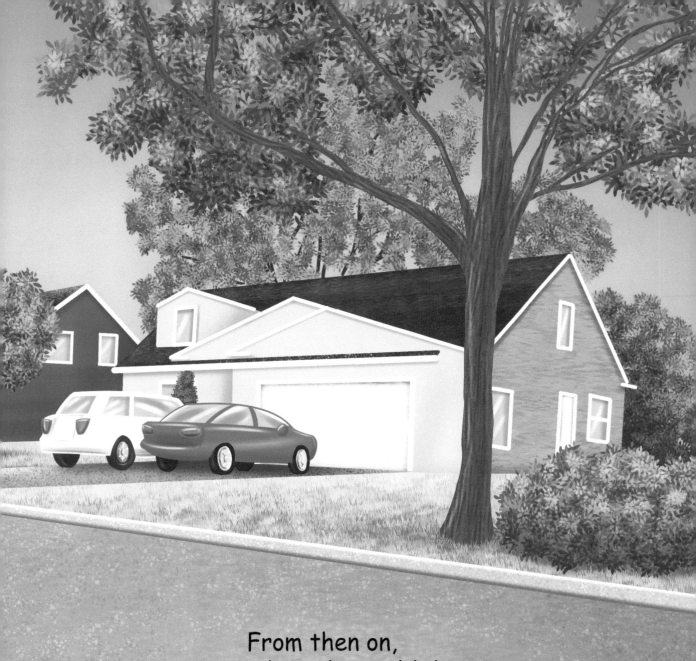

From then on,
Danny knew he could do
anything he set his mind to.
**What really mattered
was trying his best,
and he was ready
to do just that!**

Meet
Dana Reid

Dana Reid is a child psychiatrist and
children's book author. She writes stories
to inspire kids to believe in themselves,
gain confidence, overcome their fears,
and be the best version of themselves.
She lives in Milton, Georgia, with her
husband and 2 children. You can connect
with her on Instagram @drdanareid.

CPSIA information can be obtained
at www.ICGtesting.com
Printed in the USA
LVHW071512280223
740379LV00002B/2

9 781088 078082